E.T.
THE EXTRA-TERRESTRIAL

By Arie Kaplan

Illustrated by Chris Fennell

 A GOLDEN BOOK • NEW YORK

rhcbooks.com

Educators and librarians, for a variety of teaching tools, visit us at RHTeachersLibrarians.com

ISBN 978-0-593-48300-8 (trade) — ISBN 978-0-593-48301-5 (ebook)

Printed in the United States of America

10 9 8 7 6 5 4 3 2 1

Late one night, when everyone was asleep, aliens came to Earth! They studied plant life. Then they went back to their spaceship. But one little alien was left behind!

Elliott was a boy who lived with his mother, Mary, his older brother, Michael, and his younger sister, Gertie.

Elliott loved his family. But he sometimes felt left out.

Elliott discovered the alien from outer space hiding in the toolshed. He called his new friend E.T. It was short for "extra-terrestrial," which is another word for "alien"!

Elliott asked his new friend from outer space, "Can you say 'E.T.'?"

Elliott showed E.T. to Gertie and Michael. "I'm keeping him," he told them. They promised not to tell their mom.

Elliott hid E.T. in his closet.

Gertie gave the alien a flower. "A plant for you," she said.

At school, Elliott was supposed to study frogs in science class. But the frogs reminded him of E.T., so he set them free!

"I want to save you," he told the frogs.

Elliott discovered that E.T. had healing
powers. The alien made Gertie's wilting
flower bloom. And when Elliott got a cut
on his finger, E.T. made it all better!

E.T. started collecting things—toys, telephones, and other electronics—from around Elliott's house. He was building a communication device to contact his alien friends!

On Halloween, everyone went trick-or-treating. The alien was dressed as a ghost. Elliott was dressed as a classic monster. They hid E.T.'s communication device inside his costume!

Elliott took E.T. to the forest. That was where he would use his communicator to contact his alien friends.

E.T. made Elliott's bicycle fly so they would get there faster! Elliott was not used to flying. "Not so high," he told E.T.

Elliott helped E.T. activate the communicator. The machine beeped and whirred as it came to life.

It's working!

Just then, some scientists came to take E.T. away. They wanted to study him. But Elliott and his friends helped E.T. escape!

"Where are they?" the scientists asked. But it was too late. The little alien took off in an ambulance—with Elliott driving!

Then E.T. flew Elliott and his friends to the pickup spot. They could not believe they were really flying! Elliott told them that E.T.'s ship would be there soon.

The spaceship arrived to take
E.T. home. Elliott hugged his friend
goodbye.
    E.T. touched a glowing finger to Elliott's
head and said, "I'll be right here."
    He meant that Elliott would always
remember him.

Elliott was sad to see E.T. go. But the alien was right. Elliott would never forget his extra-terrestrial friend!